JESS

The Life of a Twisted Mind

B. Y. JONES

Tellwell Talent
www.tellwell.ca

ISBN
978-1-998190-25-6 (Paperback)
978-1-998190-26-3 (eBook)

ABOUT THIS BOOK

Jess is a young man who gives his all to be successful, but he is to find it is his own shortcomings that are his downfall. He loves his family and home, but is torn between his earlier life, travel, and home. He spends years looking for something. Until one day he figures it out.

This is a complete work of fiction. All names are a figment of my imagination.

PROLOGUE

Jess was a very lonely boy. His mother never let him play with the other children in his neighborhood. She said their parents were poor, and not good enough for him. When not in school, he spent all of his time in his room. When in high school, other kids scorned him and called him names. He didn't have social skills. He had a crush on a cute girl named Carol. She started talking to him one day and hinted for a date. He built up courage and asked her out. He was surprised to find that she continued to go out with him several more times. Then one day, he overheard her with her friends, saying how the bet was off, she put up with him, more then she was supposed to. He was devastated.

For my daughter Rose; for all her help and for believing in me.

CHAPTER 1

Jess led a lonely lifestyle from one-nighters to semi-meaningful relationships. Drifting from town to town and woman to woman, never receiving total satisfaction. Although you can't say, that he didn't try. He would be seen from day to day hanging around drinking establishments, never getting involved with anyone. Always searching for the woman of his dreams. One thing you could say is that Jess was loyal to whatever woman he was involved with at the time. From time to time he could be seen with a doll on his arm, showing her to the world with pride. To Jess, pride was all you needed. He had been burned many times and the way he figured, it, was a learning experience each time. He was a persistent type, never saying no and never giving up. Hoping the next time would be different.

Now at loose ends, he was playing the game of a hunter. Xandra on the other hand was the extreme opposite. She had learned early, that she could get away with a flash of her smile, and, she could reap the rewards. She had good looks, was smart, perhaps too smart, with a strong taste for success at any cost. She worked for an advertising agency. That is where they met. Jess was an architect specializing in condos. He had been working at this for two years, since college. They had shared many lunches, never daring to cross the line between business and personal affairs. They had worked together off and on for the past several months, but Jess began to feel there was something about her. He couldn't quite put his finger on it. He had watched her get into scrapes and completely enjoyed the way she could twist the facts. Escaping, showing no battle scars to the business world. Jess totally admired her.

He decided to carry on as usual and wait for the opportune time. Jess wanted her and each day that went by, it became more visible. Finally, opportunity knocked. Jess was going to his summer house near Clear Lake, Ontario, for two weeks. He would ask her, if, she would like to come with him? That evening over a candle-light dinner, he asked. He told her his idea, overflowing with the promise of tranquility and relaxation, playing against the hustle and bustle of the big city of Toronto. She didn't need much convincing, she readily accepted, offering her ideas of how to spend their time. Things were looking up for Jess, and this was the chance to see what she is really like. Of course, they agreed to keep this holiday to themselves, as neither wanted their private lives known. Trying to avoid office gossip. They arrived at the cottage Saturday evening. The moon was high, and the rain could be heard pelting against the glass of the repair riddled cottage. The nearby pier was conducting a wave-induced, seemingly well-practiced symphony. From the distance a loon could be heard, offering its, eerie call to the lake. They unpacked, and went to bed. As a lover, she told him he is incompetent, and she expected more, so he gave it, with his hands on her throat as he climaxed.

The slapping of the waves continued their unbreakable timing as if to break the silence of the night. Jess looked at his trembling hands and his boots caked in mud. He thought," if only she had listened to me!" Earlier that evening, she was laughing at him and mocking his style. Xandra had made him feel like a kid again and how different he is, and lacking in intelligence. How he lacks in social skills and can't even make love right. Nevertheless, the scene was a great blow to his pride. Even now as he thinks to himself, it was inevitable. His usually cool temper turned unexpectedly for the worse. Giving her the surprise that she'd earned. Silently, he hauled on his cigar, mentally tracing his steps, searching for possible slip-ups. Thunder clapped and through the flash of lightening he could see the fence, where she took her last crying breath. He was remembering the mixture of her blood and the smell of dry rot, ever so grateful to the rain for cleaning up his mess. Now he had to figure out what to do with her body? How would he explain of her disappearance? With these questions in mind he returned to the first problem at hand. She was still dead and lying, wrapped in a blanket, in a bundle by the fence. The dawn was now streaking through the darkness, playfully dancing on the water. He was thinking, "maybe I can get away with this, I just have to think about it. Who could have known she was with me?" He drew a blank. He then went to the shed for a spade. He walked solemnly to the garden, proceeding to dig. By noon he was finished. He went over to her corpse, slung her over his shoulder and placed her in to the very deep hole. After a few words, he covered her. The cottage was secluded, so at least he didn't have to worry about being seen. He was sorry that it ended this way but, he had his pride too. He thought to himself, "it's not much, but the best I can do." He tidied up the area and made it look as if he had done a little gardening. He rested briefly, then he returned the spade to the shed. He thought about leaving but, thought he should stay until the spring gardening was done. That way, it would look like that, was the reason why he was here. "Why did she have to demean him like she did? But she had and now she is in no condition to bargain."

CHAPTER 2

Jess stayed one more week, and was satisfied he had, all of the gardens were looking good. Jess liked everything to be perfect. He couldn't stand untidiness. He then returned to his office in Toronto. Apparently, everyone thought Xandra had extended her holiday and no one had missed her. Monday, there was a project notice on the board, it seemed that no one else wanted, so Jess checked it out. Apparently, a company in Rome, Italy, was looking for an architect. It would be a two-year contract, and relocation would be necessary. Jess thought, "perfect!!" He took the offer from the board, and approached his boss. His firm hadn't been global but, they were hoping to broaden their horizons. They talked and had agreed, that Jess was moving to Rome. He then went straight to a real estate office, and listed his condo for sale, completely furnished. All he had to do was pack his clothes and personals. He flew to Rome the next Monday. Rome was everything he thought it would be, and was so happy about the opportunity. As it turned out there was a lot of building going on. Jess called his boss in Toronto, and explained that the company in Rome, was trying new ideas, that Jess had been providing for them. This was providing an opening for the expansion that they were hoping for. After a few months, they asked if he would stay indefinitely, as they were pleased with his work. He agreed to think about it. His condo was sold in Toronto and he had hired a company to check in on his cottage near the lake, and to keep the grounds up. He sent them a key. He thought he might like to go home for a holiday next year. He would spend five or six weeks there for a break.

The year passed by quickly, as he was so busy. When he arrived in Toronto, he called in at his old office, to see if his old friend Dan was in. They had been keeping in touch. He asked Dan if he would like to accompany him to his cottage. Dan had said, "Yes, I would love to, but I can only stay for a week." Jess had rented a car, and Dan followed him. They enjoyed a great week of fishing, swimming, and barbecuing. While sitting on the patio the evening before he was leaving, Dan started to talk, keeping Jess up late with the office gossip. He brought up Xandra's name, and said that at first the talk, was that she had run away to Rome, but he had told them he kept in touch with me, and that she hadn't. Apparently she had no family, so it was assumed that she had run off with someone that she was seeing." Dan thought with her looks, it was probably what had happened. He knew money mattered with her, so she probably nabbed a rich guy. Jess felt very relieved, and he could finally relax and put it behind him for good. He felt that it was unfortunate how things had ended the way they did, but she had it coming. How dare she treat him as if he was stupid and like the girls had, in high school. When his vacation ended, he went back to Rome, planning on leaving his old life behind him for good, but two years later, he was finding his life very tedious. He was having great difficulties with the language and, as a result, not able to go out much. He found it boring just to stay in. Since his last contract wasn't quite up yet, he decided that he had to start going out more. He found what looked like a nice bar, three blocks from his apartment. He found the food was good, and sometimes they had musical groups playing for the evening. It was a very relaxing atmosphere, and he started going every night after work. Everyone was friendly, and it was always busy. One night it was especially so, and all the tables were taken. He was waiting for his food to come, when he happened to look up. He noticed an exceptionally beautiful lady had appeared. She asked if she could share his table. "Of course," he said, "please join me." She said, "thank you," and sat down. Jess introduced himself, prompting her to respond, and she said, "Hi, I'm Rebecca." Jess said, "it sure is nice to sit with someone who speaks English. Where are you from Rebecca?" She said that she was born and raised in London, England, but had moved here last year. She shared that she was having a hard time with the language too. She asked Jess where he was from? He thought for a moment, then said, "I'm from Canada, actually, Edmonton, Alberta. I also came here for work." They chatted all through the meal, and decided to meet again at the same time and place the next day. Jess left the bar thinking how good he felt, and how things were looking up.

The next day Jess arrived at six p.m., and found Rebecca already seated. She said, "Hi, is this table satisfactory?" He replied, "yes, very." When he sat down, the waitress brought menu's to them, and asked if they would like a drink before ordering? Jess replied that he would like coffee. Rebecca said that she would have the same. They had both decided on shrimp alfredo, and placed their order. While drinking coffee, they started with small talk, to get to know each other better. Rebecca asked him, what kind of work brought him to Rome? He explained that he was an architect and has a contract for some new buildings to be constructed. He told her how he really likes the work and how it challenges him. Then he asked her what she does? "I'm a freelance writer for a newspaper based in Chicago, United States. I'm here to cover a big story. It's an ongoing story that my boss needs more attention paid to. So, I'll be here for a while. Then who knows where to next? I'm afraid I can't disclose my story before publication." They had a very tasty mea, l and continued to get to know each other better. She was alone now, as her only sister had passed away with leukemia, four years earlier. Both parents were gone as well. Jess told her he was sorry, he knew how it felt to be alone, as both his parents, were gone as well. Although Jess had no idea about his parents. When he had finished school, he walked away from them and never contacted them, ever again. So, he thought it best to not say anything. After dinner they went to a theatre, then they stopped for a drink. Jess hailed a cab and took her back to her hotel. He agreed to meet her for dinner the next day, and Jess thought, I really like her, so he asked if she would like to go out again, after dinner? She said, "Yes I would love to." They went to a bar with entertainment and dancing. They discovered how much they like the same things, and had a great time. When Jess took her home, he gave her a soft kiss good night. He finally was starting to feel really good again. They continued to meet for dinner and other activities, for a couple of months.

Things were going very well, and Jess was starting to think about becoming more serious with her. At dinner on Friday, he asked her if she would like to go to a new bar that had just opened. He heard that it has a nice band and dancing. She looked happy when he asked her, and she said, "yes." Jess thought to himself, it's time to ask her to move in with him. They had danced to almost every song and Jess thought that we are a perfect match. He took his leave to visit the washroom, and to ask her, when he returned. He came out of the washroom, and was about to go back to the booth. When he noticed that she was talking to someone who was sitting at their table. He approached them slowly, and sat behind her in the next booth. He was stunned when he heard what she was saying, so he sat still and listened. Rebecca was telling her friend about how Jess was such a jerk. With his money, and obviously, he had lots, she was going to marry him, no matter what it takes, to make it happen. Then everything would be hers. She was sure that in two years, she could clean him out. Jess thought, "I can't believe this scheme of hers. I'm well off, but not rich." Jess slowly got up and walked out the door. He needed time to think. He never would have expected, what he had just heard. He realized what a fool he had been, Jess decided to just walk away and get on with his life. He tried to block his mind but, found it hard to do. He thought, "why am I such a target?" He found a new restaurant a few streets away, and never expected to see her again. He was so glad he hadn't taken her to his apartment, so she didn't know where he lived. However, she wasn't about to let him go. She started searching for him. Jess was sitting at the back table, eating a very nice spaghetti dinner, when she came in. He sat quietly and hoped that she wouldn't see him, but of course she did. It was obvious she was looking for him. She had been searching for days. She approached his table, and asked if she could sit down. He told her that it has been fun, but that he doesn't want a serious relationship. She looked at him and said, "Me neither, I just want to be friends. I miss having my meals with you. Please, may I sit down?" Jess knew that she was lying, so he said, "No, we are finished." She said, "You will regret this, I am not done with you." The next day when Jess was leaving his office, he saw her talking to his boss. When she left, he asked his boss, "what was she doing here?" His boss said, "Asking about you. I told her any questions about you, that she needs to ask you." I told my boss how she had appeared at the restaurant last night, and insisted on sitting with me. I told her that I didn't know her and told her to sit elsewhere. Now she is here, and there is obviously something wrong with her." He agreed. The only information she had of Jess, was where he worked so, she figured that if she could become a nuisance, she could get him back. Jess decided that he had better do something, or it was going to become worse. So, the next time Rebecca appeared at his table, he asked her to join him. She met him every night for the next two weeks. Then Jess invited her to go to the movies with him, after dinner one night. It had been fairly pleasant, so he asked her to go to the bar with him, on Monday after dinner. She said she would, and gave him a sly little grin. He knew, she was thinking about how she was succeeding with her plan. Jess thought, "Aha! She thinks she's caught me in her web but, I think I'll catch her in mine."

On Monday before dinner, Jess parked his car on the hill overlooking his last project in Rome. He often sat here looking at the gorgeous view, and knew that soon he would never be seeing it again, because of the massive building he had designed. He took a shovel from the trunk, and walked down the small hill to the forms of the basement. In the morning they would be covered in cement. The ground was soft, due to the preparations. So, in no time at all, he had dug a very deep hole. He went back to his car working out his plan, of a few drinks and dancing, followed by him asking if she would like to see his building project? It worked brilliantly. She of course told him she would love to, as she had been wondering about it for a while now. She knew his work was more than just sitting at a desk. They had arrived at the hill, and she was astounded by the view. Jess thought, she must be a good actress, because from what he had overheard, no way, she would care about a view. Jess thought that because of her plan, she was cold and unfeeling. A gold digger as well. He pulled a bottle of wine from the back seat and said, "Follow me." She exclaimed, "A picnic, Oh Yes!" They went down the slope and he spread the blanket out. When they sat down, he poured them each some wine. He knew that she liked wine, and she swallowed it right down. He poured her another and as she sipped this one, he was holding her hand and gently rubbing her arm. Then his hand slipped into her blouse, and she gently kissed him. This let him know that she was willing, so he proceeded to do more feeling and groping. She gulped down the rest of her wine, as he was unfastening her pants. He inched them down, as she reached over and undid his fly and reached in for him. When they were basically bottomless, he flipped her onto her knees and said, "Let's start this way." She said, "I have never done it this way before, but I will go for the ride." She was thinking, this is so good, I might have to keep him for more than two years. When Jess felt he was ready to ejaculate, he reached up and rubbed her neck, and as the pleasure built, he started to squeeze. She was pinned under him, so she couldn't move, or breathe, unable to speak or scream. She felt the blackness overtake her, as her breath left her. When he was finished, so was she. He wrapped her and her clothing in the blanket, making sure he didn't miss anything. He carried her to the hole he had dug earlier. He was intent on cleaning up the surroundings, making sure everything went in. After putting her in it, he filled it, meanwhile, thinking she would be covered in cement soon. He returned the shovel to the work-shed and went back to his car. He then went home and changed his soiled clothes. He went to a coffee shop to kill some time and be seen. He bought a coffee to go, and returned to the hill. There he sat in his car, and waited for the cement trucks to come. He didn't have long to wait. When they covered where she lay and part of the floor, he started his car and drove away. He had packed up, signed out of his work and condo the day before, so he headed for the airport. His boss had asked him to sign onto another contract, but he had told him that he needed a break. He would go home for a bit but, would be in touch. At the airport, he turned in his rental car and boarded a plane for London, England.

CHAPTER 3

Jess arrived at London's airport on a cold January afternoon. On the long flight, he found that he couldn't slow his mind down. He kept wondering, what is wrong with me? Why don't women like me? They seem to be only interested in my money and financial position. I'm good-looking, with my blond hair, blue eyes and six foot two-inch height, I work out regularly, and am in great shape. Why couldn't Rebecca have cared for me? I thought we had a great connection, until I heard her in the bar. I guess I should count myself lucky to be out of that trap.

He rented a car, and drove toward the middle of London. It looked to be the the oldest part, with no new buildings to be seen. Jess was surprised that he felt so relaxed, as he was used to new and larger buildings. He found it felt like home, and found a hotel to settled in, went to the dining area, and enjoyed a nice meal. He noticed most of the menu consisted of an assortment of fish. Most, he had never tried before, and he hadn't recognized the name of the dish he had ordered, but it was very good. He thought, I might really like it here. Satiated, he went up to his room, to bed. He would explore tomorrow. The next morning, he had another first... kippers for breakfast. He thought, how different. He decided to go out and look around, see if he might stay for a while. After walking for some distance, he stopped at a bar not far from the London Bridge, and ordered ale and a sandwich for lunch. An older gentleman sat down beside him and started some small talk. After a while it became apparent, that they had similar interests. The man introduced himself as Dave Wilson. Jess shook his hand and introduced himself. Jess told him that he had just arrived, and was an architect, and is looking for work. Dave said, "Isn't that interesting, I have a contract to design and remodel a bunch of houses, and I'm looking for someone who knows about such things." They discussed ideas and wages, and Jess found himself employed. So he guessed that he would stay a while. Jess was to meet Dave at the first project the next morning. Jess thought, great, no contract, no visa, perfect, I can leave whenever I like.

Three months later, Jess was beginning to think about moving on. It was a nice place to live, and the women there were refreshing and not clingy, but he felt something was still missing. He went to Dave to explain, how he has enjoyed working with him, but he was missing home. He told Dave that he would leave all his housing plans, so it would be easy for the work to continue with his crew. Dave reluctantly agreed, and said that he would miss him. The next day, Jess boarded a plane for home. He had been gone four years.

CHAPTER 4

He arrived in Toronto at ten that night. It felt good to be home. He rented a car and headed for the 401 Highway. By eleven, he was at a coffee shop about an hour from his summer home. It felt good to be back but, he was getting very tired. He had arrived about midnight, but there was a car in the driveway and all lights were out. He wondered about the car in the driveway, so he cautiously, used his key and went in and turned the lights on. He was tired, and nothing seemed wrong so he went straight to his bedroom and opened the door. A woman screamed. Jess's first thought was, what the hell? Then a man jumped up demanding to know who he was? What are you doing here? Jess replied, "I own this house, and I want to know, what you are doing here?" The man replied, "I look after this house for Mr. Collins." Jess spoke up and said, "Well, I'm Jess Collins and I never said you could live here. How long has this been going on?" The man replied, "just this summer, so I can keep up with repairs." Jess said, "get out of bed, and both of you be out of here in twenty minutes. You can give me my key at the door, where I will be waiting." When they had gone, Jess locked up and left for a motel. Even though he was tired, there was no way he was sleeping in that bed. He had never had anyone spend a night with him in his bed. So, no way in hell, would he sleep after someone else. The next day he went to a new and used furniture store on highway twenty -eight. He bought a new bed, sheets and blankets. They agreed to buy his old ones and he gave them an extra hundred dollars to deliver and pick up the old bed, that day. He returned to his house to wait. He stripped the bed and emptied the dressers into garbage bags. The furniture arrived after lunch, and they replaced the bed, and then loaded the old one onto the truck. Jess asked if they knew where he could get rid of some of the old clothes? They told him they would take care of it. He took time to clean and make up the bed and unpack, ready for night. Finally, he was home and could relax.

A week later he was sitting with a beer, just before dark, when there was a knock at his door. When he opened it, he found the woman he had put out with his gardener. She said, "Hi, my name is Sandra Long but, everyone calls me Sandy. I'm sorry to bother you, but I felt the need to explain. I didn't know that this wasn't

Dave's house. I feel really bad, and I am so sorry." She seemed really sincere, so Jess asked if she would like to join him for a beer? She said that she would love to. After talking for a while, it seemed like they had a lot in common. She seemed to like Jess as much as he liked her. They went for a moon-light swim, nude of course, as she didn't have a suit with her. Jess never wore one. After, instead of getting dressed, they went to bed. They continued like that for the rest of the summer. Jess found he had a strange feeling, and that something was missing, but he thought maybe he was just tired. He told Sandra that he has a job coming up in September, in Texas. Even though it seemed something was missing, he asked if Sandy would like to go with him? She said, "No, I am a teacher at the university not far from here. I must start back at the end of August. It's a good job and I love it." Jess thought, "When was she going to tell me? Was she just going to walk out?" He told her, "That's good. Why don't we meet here next summer?" She told him that she couldn't as she had agreed to go on a trip with her mother. So Jess told her he would probably just work through then. Maybe if she was to be free, they could hook up the following summer? Sandra replied, "Maybe.' Jess decided that he would be here. Possibly, he would meet someone else to bring.

Summer ended and they both went on their way. Jess worked a hard winter in Texas, when speaking to his boss in March, he had set up a three-week vacation, to go home in July. He realized that he needed the break. He flew home again, and the long drive from Toronto, left him tired as usual. When he pulled in his driveway, again, he found a car parked there. His first thought was, Sandy must have changed her plans. He went in and, again, he found Sandy and Dave in his bed. He hit the overhead light switch, and they both jumped up. He said, "So, now I see what's going on, Sandy you are really the one living in my house, and he's your entertainment." She said, "well, it does get lonely with you gone." Jess asked what happened to her trip? She said that it got cancelled. Jess said, "Why didn't you call me then?" She indicated that she didn't want to bother him while at work, and that he told her that he wouldn't be coming until next year. So Jess said, "Okay this is ending right now." He had them each put on a robe. He had them put their hands behind their backs, and tied the belts at the front. The only threat, Jess could see was Dave. So, since Jess was much bigger and stronger than Dave was he tied his hands first, by pulling the ties of the robe to the back and around his wrists. He then tied Sandy the same way. Then he tied the ends of the sleeves to the back as well, making them very secure. Sandy asked what he was doing as she couldn't move. He told her that she wouldn't have it on for long. Jess took them outside, steering them towards the lake. He told them to get in the boat. Sandy could only get in with his help. Jess rowed way out onto the lake and told Dave to stand up. After untying him, and before untying the sleeves, Jess pulled the tie off and tied it around his ankles. Then he removed the robe. Dave asked, "What are you doing?" Jess said, me, nothing, you, however, are going for a nude moon-light swim." He then pushed Dave into the water. Dave was not a good swimmer, so Jess said, "I'd better help". So he placed the end of the paddle on Dave's head and held him down. After a few minutes, Dave stopped struggling. Sandy started talking, because she knew that she would be next. But Jess told her to shut up. He took her robe off and pushed her in. She was a better swimmer, so he jumped in and held her arms so she couldn't get free. It wasn't long until he felt the life leave her. He then collected all parts of the robes and placed them in the boat, as if they had stepped out of them. He then left the boat and swam to the shore. His suitcase was still in the trunk, so he changed into dry clothes and headed to the coffee shop, near the university. He sat quietly with a coffee, and then ordered one to go. He went to the hotel that he usually stopped at. The next morning, he stopped in town and bought his new bedding and groceries, then returned home. He carried everything in and changed the bed, putting the used items in the laundry hamper. He called the police to report a strange car in his driveway.

When the officer arrived, he explained that he had just got home from working in Texas and that he had no idea whose car it was, or why it was here. As the officer was getting in his car, he had received a call on his radio. It had appeared that they had two bodies had been found floating in the lake near a boat. The officer exited his car and asked Jess if he had a boat? Jess told him, "Yes, it's out in the back." They went to the back where it should have been, only to discover that it was gone. Jess told the officer that he had just got back from Texas, and was on holiday for three weeks. Jess explained that he hadn't even had time to unpack yet. His suitcase and groceries were still in the kitchen. The officer went in and looked to see if Jess was right. He saw the groceries but, he noticed the cupboards and refrigerator were full of food. When they went into the bedroom, they saw the clothes. The officer said, "It appearsthat they were living in your house. Had you loaned or rented to them?" Jess said that he had not. "I don't even know who they are?" The officer then asked if there was somewhere he could stay?, as this is now a crime scene. Jess agreed to go back to the motel where he had stayed the prior night. When the officer came to the motel the next day, he told Jess that everything he had said yesterday, checked out. The couple had apparently seen that the cottage was empty, so they had moved in. They had probably drowned while having a midnight swim. One probably took a cramp panicked, and took the other one down too. The officer said, "I have just one question, how did they open the door? It doesn't look to be tampered with. Does anyone else have a key?" Jess told him, yes, that he had been paying a young man, Dave, to trim the grass and check on things. The officer asked if Dave had a last name? Jess told him, "Dave Marley." The officer said, "Well there you go, the man found in the lake was identified as Dave Marley. That is his car in your driveway, which is being moved at this moment." He told Jess that he could move back into his home by this evening, and the car and clothing were being removed. Jess did move back that night, however, he decided to go back to Texas the next day. Jess was feeling very restless and no longer wanted to vacation.

CHAPTER 5

Jess arrived in Dallas, Texas, the next day. He went straight to his room at the hotel where he had been staying. His room was still available, so he unpacked and went to bed. He was exhausted. The next morning, while having his breakfast in the dining room, he began thinking about staying longer than he had originally planned. He began searching for a condo that he could rent. He bought a local paper and checked the listings. There was one listed three blocks from his office, so he called the agent. Jess arranged for a viewing after lunch. It turned out to be everything he was looking for, and he rented it. He could move in immediately, as it was already empty. By nine that night he was moved in, and the refrigerator and cupboards were well stocked. He decided to go out for a drink at the bar down the street. He found a bar called "The Flamingo" very pleasant and it had live entertainment. It seemed to be a friendly place, and everyone appeared to know each other. He found himself being welcomed into the group. When he started to feel tired, he said his goodnights, explaining his jet-lag. Jess told them he would probably be back the next night. The next morning, he decided to explore the big city. He stopped at a café for lunch. It was a quiet district, not far from where the Rodeo was held. Jess had just ordered lunch, when an older man came in. He looked tired, and stressed. The café was full, and the man was told that he would have to wait or come back. Jess had overheard, and since he was alone at the table, he interjected and asked if the man would like to share his table? The man sat down, thanked Jess, and put his hand out. With a grin he said, "Hi, I'm Jake Turner." Jess shook his hand and said, "Hi, I'm Jess Collins." When the food came, they were already in the middle of pleasant conversation. Jake was saying how he raises Arabian horses for racing, and has twenty new ones coming in next month. He had been looking for someone to draft plans for a new barn. He would like training and housing to take place in one building, throughout the long winters. Jess, told Jake, "Well, I am on holiday, so could I possibly assist you?" Jess then explained that he is an architect and had just moved here, about a year ago and who he is employed with. Jake told him that he was impressed and would gladly pay whatever this work is worth. He also told him that he was getting desperate, as he has tried everywhere, and everyone is booked until next year, including your employer. Since Jess had nothing pressing to do, he followed Jake to his ranch. For Jess it was love at first sight… the house, the gardens, the barns, and the magnificent horses. Jake showed him where he wanted to erect a new barn. Then he invited him in for coffee. Jess asked for a paper and pen. He sat as they had coffee and listened to Jake talk about his dream for his barn. With coffee done and getting ready to leave, Jess handed Jake the paper. He asked him, "Is this what you had in mind?" Jake took the paper and with excitement said, "Exactly!" Jess took the paper back and asked questions about size and other particulars. He told Jake, he would be back the next day with completed plans. Before he left, he told Jake to start looking for a building crew. They shook hands and Jess left. When Jess returned with completed plans and a list of materials needed, Jake invited him to come back for dinner that night, with a bill for his services. When Jess came back at six for dinner, Jake told him, "The materials are ordered and a crew has been hired to start construction on Monday." He asked Jess for his invoice and had his checkbook out, but Jess said, "I would much rather keep you as a friend, since I don't know anyone here, so no charge." Jess explained to him, that it is easy to draw up plans quickly for a barn. A barn is mostly walls, a roof and dividers. So, I am happy to do this." They shook hands, and Jess followed him to the dining room. They just sat down when this stunning woman came in. She was perfect in every way. He stood up and Jake introduced his daughter, Amy. It was a lovely dinner of roast chicken with all the trimmings. The crème brulee' dessert was to die for. Jess realized he could fall madly in love with Amy. He had never felt this strongly before, so fast. He really hoped she felt the instant magnetism as well.

CHAPTER 6

Jess found that he really had enjoyed hanging out at the ranch. When his holiday was over and he went back to work, he found it very stressful. He was longing for the ranch. He spent all his weekends there, and Amy showed him how to ride and care for horses. He learned how to clean stalls, feed, and groom the horses. He never thought that he would like something so much. He watched the new barn being built and now he realized, how much it was needed. He joined Jake at the racetrack every chance he got, and learned which horses were the best to bet on. For the next year, he became a regular at the track and very seldom lost. Between work and betting, he was growing his funds rapidly.

Jess found Amy beautiful in both looks and personality. Actually, he couldn't fault her in any way. She was honest, sensual, energetic and more than he ever could have imagined possible in a woman. He knew that he could easily spend the rest of his life with her. She was five foot nine inches tall, considered tall for a woman, however, she still seemed short beside him. A perfect fit. She had lovely, long, dark hair, with a natural wave. Her eyes were blue, and he felt he could drown in them. She is a certified accountant, and works in an office in Dallas. She is successful and proficient. Jess felt he could relax, because she was more than his equal financially. They had become best friends. Jess asked Amy if she would go out with him on a date?, and her answer was, "Yes, what took you so long?" He was relieved that apparently, she had been waiting for him to ask. They started dating, went to the theatre weekly, the rodeo and basically everywhere, when they weren't working.

Jess and Amy were getting very close and he knew they were right for each other. He proposed to her and she said, "Yes." They planned the wedding to be next June. In March after much discussion with Amy, he decided to sell his cottage near Lakeview, back in Ontario. Amy told him that she would like to see it before he sells it. So he made plans for a trip in two-weeks time. When they arrived, they checked everything out, as he hadn't been back for two years. Amy cleaned the inside, while Jess cut the grass and tidied the gardens. Two days later, they called a realtor, and the house was listed and sold by the next weekend. Amy thought it was sad to let it go but, it wasn't practical to keep it. They flew home the day after the closure was finalized. Jess was feeling relief and happy, and finally having closure with his old life. He has hopes that he can finally have the life and family that had he always wanted.

CHAPTER 7

June came and Jake insisted on giving them the best wedding ever. He was well-known, and invited everyone. The lawn and gardens were filled with tents and tables, with five hundred guests in attendance. Jess met neighbours and co-workers of Amy's. He had made many friends at the race track, and they also came to share in his day. All food and drinks were catered, so it was a great time. Too soon, it was time for the happy couple to leave, for their honey-moon.

The honeymoon ended and life resumed. After thirty days away, they had much to catch up on. The big decision was where to live? They both preferred the ranch, however, it was her dad's ranch. Jess suggested, they look for a ranch for sale, and make a start for themselves. Jess went online, and found a ranch for sale in Alberta, Canada. He still had his Canadian citizenship, so Amy agreed they could go to see it.

Jess found the ranch, about one hour north of Lethbridge, located along the Oldman River. It would take a day to drive there, so he suggested they take two weeks when they drive out to see it. They left on Saturday, taking their time, and enjoying the scenes along the way. Upon arrival, they called the realtor, who was expecting them.

He agreed to take them for a viewing after lunch. They met with him and went to see, what they had hoped would be their new home. It turned out to be everything they were looking for. The view of the river and bridge were breathtaking. It turned out that the rail-bridge was the longest and tallest in the world, built in 1909. They went back to the realty office and signed the papers. It would be theirs' in sixty days. They stayed the rest of the week to become familiar with the area.

Upon arrival home, Jake was anxiously awaiting them. They told him, what they had purchased, and showed him the brochures. He was sad, that they would be moving, but, happy for them. At least they weren't moving that far. Since he, went back and forth to the rodeo all the time.

Moving day came and they had packed everything that they were taking. They had borrowed Jake's pickup truck and trailer, as Amy was taking her two horses. Jake was to drive Amy's car up in a few days, and drive his truck and trailer home. Jess and Amy would have to go shopping as soon as arriving, since they only took clothes and personals with them. They took turns driving and resting, but it was a straight through drive. They left at six a.m. Monday morning, and arrived at 4p.m.

Amy settled her horses into the stalls in the barn, and fed and watered them. Jess unhooked the trailer and they left for town. They bought take-out for supper and then found a furniture store. They purchased a five-piece bedroom set for their bedroom and a three piece for the guest room. Delivery was set for the next day. They went to the hardware store and purchased paint. They bought four gallons of pale blue for the bedrooms, and six gallons of white for kitchen, halls, and dining room. Since the house came with all appliances, they went for groceries next. When they unloaded the truck, they spread blankets on the living room rug; tonight's bed. After a couple of hours rest, they started painting bedrooms and the upstairs halls, before giving in to sleep. The next day after everything arrived and was set up, they went to town for bedding and furniture for the living and dining rooms. They asked for it not to be delivered until next week, painting would be done by then. Shopping was done for now, they could go home. They spent the rest of the day with the horses.

Saddled up, they went exploring. The horses adapted quickly to their new home.

After all the work of moving was done, Jess decided to hire some help for the ranch. He went online, and posted a help wanted ad for a ranch foreman and a cook-housekeeper. Amy had placed an order at the hardware store for needs in the barn, and asked if he could pick them up? Jess left at once. While at the store, he met the owner, and explained that they had bought the Circle C Ranch. Jess told him that they won't be changing the name of the ranch, because, my name is Jess Collins, and Circle C still works. He told him that he and Amy had just moved from a big ranch in Texas, owned by her father Jake Turner. The owner said, "Does he race thoroughbreds?" Jess told him,"'Yes." He replied, "When you see him, tell him Gus Whiley says, hi." They shook hands and Gus thanked him for his business. He also told him that it is good to have new people in the area and if there was is anything he can do for them, to let him know? Jess said, "Actually there is, if you know anyone looking for work, I need a foreman and a house-keeper cook." Gus said, "I do know a young woman, who lost her husband in an accident two years ago, and is still struggling. She could use the work, however, she has a small child about four, if that is all right with you? I can give you her number." Jess said, "Yes, she sounds perfect." He called her right awayand she was interested. They arranged for a meeting the next day at the ranch. She arrived for the interview, bringing her son with her. Amy met with her and liked her on sight. Her son was on his best behaviour and was adorable. Amy hired her on the spot, and asked her if she could start tomorrow? Her name was Alice Pruid, and she said she could start now, if that is alright. Amy said, "Yes!" and gave her a grand tour of the house. Amy let her know exactly what was expected of her. Alice asked if Amy would like tea, before going to the stable? Amy said, yes, but only if Alice would join her, so they could get to know each other better. Of course, there was milk and cookies for her son, Jamie. Amy learned Alice's husband was in a deadly car crash, two years earlier but, because it was determined that he had caused the crash, she received no compensation. She was behind in rent and other bills, and was looking for a new home that she can afford. Amy asked if she objected to living on the job? Alice said, "No, but, until I've saved enough to pay my overdue bills, I can't afford to pay much." Amy said, "Why don't you leave that to me and depending on how you work out, we will be reasonable. Would you mind the cottage just over from the barn?" Alice said that she and Jamie would love that. So Amy told her, it's all set then, move in when it's convenient for you. Here are your keys, let us know if you need help moving as we still have my fathers' truck until next week. Alice prepared a very nice meal for them before she left. Amy thought, this is going to work out just fine.

Alice and Jamie were moved in by the weekend and everything was going well. Jess went to the kitchen for a coffee and overheard Jamie whining to his mother that he wanted to go outside and play. She told him that she couldn't right now, as she has work to do. Go get your blocks and play with them for a while. He said, "I'm tired of playing with them." Jess walked in and asked Alice if he could speak with her for a moment? She joined him in the hall and he said, "If it's alright with you, I'm going to town and I could take Jamie with me? I will be a couple of hours, would that be okay?" She looked relieved, and said, "Yes, that would be fine." So he had his coffee, and took Jamie with him. Jess went to the hardware store to pick up some items for Amy and while he was there he noticed, Jamie didn't have a hat, so he bought him one. Jamie was so excited that he wanted to show everyone. Jess was also excited. He had never shopped with a little boy before. Jess looked at the board with articles for sale. He found a truck and trailer listed, and when he asked Gus about it, he was told it had belonged to his farm, and was a good deal. So Jess called the number and checked it out before going back home. It was in very good condition and the trailer would transfer two horses, exactly what he was looking for. He bought them and said he would have to come back to get them. He took Jamie for ice cream and headed home. Jess was elated at how things were coming together and thoroughly enjoyed the time spent with Jamie. He would ask Alice if he could spend time with Jamie around the ranch, and give her a break, as he was such a good kid. She agreed, so Jamie would become his sidekick. Amy went with him to pick up the truck and trailer. They were quite happy with the deal he had made. Now all they need is more horses.

Jake arrived in Amy's car on Friday evening. He pulled in just in time for dinner. He was surprised at how set up they were. On Saturday, Jess took Jake to the hardware store to see Gus. While they were talking, Jake happened to mention that they were looking for horses. Gus told them about an auction coming up next week, near Calgary, by the racetrack. They said their goodbye's and on the way home, Jake asked, if, Jess didn't mind, could he stay and go with them? Jess said, "Of course you can."

Amy, Jess and Jake went to the auction and Amy bought two mares that she had been wanting. Jake bought one, to take back with him. When they got back to the ranch, they unloaded the trailers and got the horses settled in. Jake informed them that he is going home, and would be leaving in the morning, and would stop to see Gus on the way to thank him for everything. Jess informed Amy that he was leaving in two days, for three months. She wasn't happy about it, but knew it had to be. She had closed her office when she moved, and he had stayed off work a long time to help get her set up. Amy drove him to the airport, and he left for Toronto to design a new plaza. Jess arrived and he couldn't believe the way his life had been, before Amy and the ranch. He was already lonely. He thought, "Best to keep busy," that way the time will seem to pass faster. He got busy and sure enough he finished a week early. Jess had called Amy every evening, but, on this call, he told her he would be coming home and landing at about two p.m. the next day, and could she arrange to pick him up? He could hear the excitement in her voice. He didn't sleep much that night, but was on time for his flight. While on the way home he did a lot of serious thinking. He had decided to reach out locally for work, meet with contractors and offer his services. He also realized, that he even missed the constant chatter of Jamie following him everywhere.

CHAPTER 8

Jake was at the airport to meet him. He told Jess that he sensed Amy wasn't well and had come to visit with her. Jess thanked him, and hoped she was just missing him. Dinner was ready when they reached the ranch, so there was only time for a quick hello. After dinner, they went to the living room to talk. Amy was first, and said, "I have news, I wanted to tell everyone together, I am pregnant. In six months, we will have a little girl." She hadn't expected such a reaction. Jess jumped up, grabbed her, kissed her and swung her around. Then abruptly put her down, saying, "Oh no, I didn't hurt you, did I?" Amy hadn't expected such a reaction. With everything happening so fast, she hadn't had time to discuss kids with Jess. Then Jake jumped up, and did the same thing. She couldn't believe how happy they were. Jess then told her his plans about working locally. He wouldn't make as much money but, they could be together. Amy and Jake both agreed it was a good plan. They thought about how good everything was turning out.

After a few days, Jake left for home, and everything returned to normal. Jess posted his job proposition on the board at Gus's hardware store and had started an online app, now it was just a waiting game. In the meantime, he did everything he could to lessen Amy's workload.

Finally small jobs started coming in and Amy was getting closer to the delivery date. One month left. Jess was glad it was spring, and work was starting to pick up. When warmer weather comes in, he would get more work especially on local ranches. That would help to keep him home.

CHAPTER 9

The waiting is over, Amy gave birth to a healthy, baby girl on April 15. She weighed 7lbs. Jess was feeling so elated and had called Jake as soon as her labor had started. Of course he came to their home, Amy's hospital visit was short, and both very proud men took her and baby home. Jess found that Alice was the perfect help for Amy. This was good, because he was getting very busy with work.

A year later, Jess was sitting in the livingroom with a coffee. Amy and Alice were chatting about some project, when Jess noticed Jamie sitting in the floor, teaching Katie, how to build with blocks. He was treating her like a sister. Jess thought, what a great kid, Jamie is.

Summer came and went, then Amy told Jess that she is pregnant again. Jess thought how blessed we are. She didn't ask if it was, boy or girl this time. She thought that a surprise would be nice. Jess agreed but, secretly, he was hoping, for a "Boy!" When the time came, it was another girl, Elizabeth Ellen, and would be called, Beth. She weighed in at 8lbs. and was healthy. Jess didn't let his disappointment show. After all Jamie is like a son to him. Jake had to come to the home again and stayed a few weeks. After Jake left, things fell into a routine once again. They were very busy and time seemed to fly by.

CHAPTER 10

Two years later, the girls were two and four and Jamie was nine. Amy felt it was time for her to go back to work. She went online and posted that she was starting a new riding school. Juniors 9 a.m. and seniors 1 p.m. to 4 p.m. It wasn't long until people started to book. She arranged to pay extra funds to Alice, who had agreed to sit for her. Amy became very busy, but she was happy. Amy asked Jess if he could build two or more cabins, so she could start a weekend getaway with trail rides? He approved and said that he would. Jess was happy that Amy was happy, and he now has the life that he always wanted. If only he could be busier. He still has that lost feeling.

With the cabins done and the weekend getaway posted online, Jess advertised for more help. He interviewed and hired, June Anders, for the kitchen assistant and cleaning, much-needed help for Alice. He also hired Ed Donner as a ranch foreman. He was experienced and when younger, had worked on this very ranch. Over the next year, Jess found the new help was working very well. With the three new cabins, the first weekend in June was booked full. Ed accompanied Amy on the trail rides, and Alice and June prepared excellent meals, all weekend long. It was a huge success. In November, Alice announced that she and Ed, were to be married in one month. She asked if it would be alright if Ed moved into their cabin? Amy and Jess were in total agreement. So, things were really working out for everyone.

CHAPTER 11

The years passed, and Jess couldn't believe, Katy was graduating high school and had been accepted at university. Jamie had just graduated and was now a veterinarian. In two years, Beth would be graduating as well. My family is almost grown, he thought, and Jess was sad. The girls had started dating and he watched them closely. The thing he didn't expect to see, was how the girls treated their dates. He realized it was normal for the girls to be in control. His daughters were no different than the girls he had dated. He thought Amy had probably been that way as well, until she had found true love. Jess came to the realization of what he had done. He now felt very guilty. Jess realized, in watching his daughters and how they reacted to boys that it was really a way of protecting themselves from being hurt, while they learned about life and the way things should be. Jess was truly shaken by this, as he realized what he had done. He now felt very guilty. Amy noticed that he seemed depressed, and asked if there was anything she could do? He said, "No, I am just very tired." Amy suggested that he take some time off, and maybe, they could go somewhere? Jess thought that was a good idea. Since it was winter and work was slack. He thought some sun would be nice. He booked them a flight to California and a room in an upscale resort for two weeks.

After a glorious two weeks and upon returning home, Amy noticed that he looked Better, but sensed something was still bothering him.

One month later Jess went to work in two towns away from home, he stopped at a bar for a drink. A lovely woman came in. She wasn't extremely nice looking, but she dressed well. It made him take notice. She sat at the bar beside him and ordered a drink. They casually started talking and Jess realized, how much he was missing his old life. How dull his life had become, and how sad he had been lately. Maybe he hadn't been wrong. Maybe it was just his changed lifestyle. He now realized, how much he had missed. Jess liked her very much, so they moved to a table and the conversation continued. Finally she yawned and said, "It's getting late, I think I'll see if there is a room available?" She returned minutes later and said, "I got one." Jess said, "Would you mind if I join you?" Her name was Selina, and she said, "I was hoping so."

They had a delightful night and it seemed they were good together, however, as it turned out, they were both married. They parted ways in the morning. It seemed they were both looking for something. Jess still felt something was missing, and now he feels even more guilty. When he returned home, Amy never asked why he hadn't come home? She just assumed that he was delayed with work. More guilt for Jess.

Jess was doing a lot of thinking and he decided, that maybe, he just missed travelling. He started taking jobs further from home. Over the next two years, he was away more then he was home. Amy was busy with the ranch and never really noticed. Two days away turned into four or five. Jess was very tired, but he managed to go to a bar every night, when away. He often picked up a lady for the night, however, he still felt something was missing. He finally realized how tired he was getting from all of the travel. He really missed Amy, and the girls and the ranch. He thought about it, and decided to go home and take some time off, stay home for a while.

CHAPTER 12

When he arrived home, he explained to Amy how he is taking a break from work. He said, "I am very tired and really needing a break." She insisted that he go to the family doctor for a checkup. Two days later, he was in the doctor's office for the result of tests. The doctor told him that he is suffering from over-work and stress. He was unable to find anything else wrong with him. He gave Jess a prescription for extra strength stress medication, to assisting him to relax. Jess had never taken anything before, and he was even upset about that. Jess went home and explained to Amy what the doctor had said. She agreed he had been working too hard. Jess told her he is going upstairs to take his first pill, and lie down until dinner. She said, "Okay, that's probably best." Jess went upstairs with a glass of water, and sat on the side of the bed. He then took the whole bottle of pills while thinking, "It's probably for the best. Those girls didn't deserve to die. There was nothing wrong with them. It is me. It is the thrill of the kill that I've been missing."

EPILOGUE

When the funeral was over and all had settled down again, Amy felt distraught and lost. Her world had fallen apart. Katy and Beth were now nineteen and twenty-one, Beth just finishing her last year of college. Alice and Ed were married and Jamie took over Ed's cottage. He was running his veterinarian business from there, as he dealt mostly with large animals. Jake had come home to be with his girls and is preparing to go home tomorrow. Amy was still feeling a huge loss, and she made Ed the manager over the trail rides, and ranch. She asked Alice to manage the bookings and everything else. Amy also hired a new young woman, Janis Moore to help. Since Ed and Alice are running things now, Amy and the girls were free to leave with Jake, and head to Texas for the summer.

Amy, Katy and Beth arrived with Jake in Texas. Amy couldn't believe, how good it felt to be home. They settled in, and she decided to go for a ride around the ranch. The girls were relaxing and tired from the long drive. Amy relaxed best on the back of a horse, and that's where she did her best thinking. She felt so alone and missed Jess terribly. She can't help but wonder why, why he would take his own life?

It was nearing the end of summer, whe, she got a visit from a detective. He stated that he had come from Canada, and was investigating an incident concerning a cottage near Clear Lake in Ontario. He said, "Apparently, your husband had owned it about twenty years ago." Amy said, "Yes that is right." The investigator then asked if he could speak with Jess?" Amy informed him that Jess had passed, and could she help him? He told her, "He was investigating a cold case. Apparently a body of a young woman was found. The owners of the cottage had decided to build a garage, and apparently a body was found when excavation started. D.N.A. tests were performed and found it is the body of Xandra Pentley, who went missing about thirty five years ago. She was known to have been dating your husband." Amy then said, "I have no idea, I hadn't met my husband then and he never mentioned anyone by that name. I met some previous friends, but no women. I went with him to sell the cottage and he told me about the couple who had been living in it, without permission and how they had drowned." He said, "About that, the D.N.A. shows there was force used, they didn't just drown, they were held under." A witness also came forward. He had been only seventeen at the time, and was afraid to come forward. He has since given a description, that matches your husband. Amy couldn't believe what she was hearing. Could Jess have been responsible? It didn't make sense, he was such a loving, caring person. The investigator then asked about Jess working in Rome. Had he known a woman, Rebecca Lindsay? Amy said, "I don't know, but she provided him with names of everyone she had met through Jess."

After the investigator left, Amy began to understand, why there were no past women in Jess' life. She wondered what was different about her, that she had survived. She now knew why he had taken his life. Why he had been so depressed. He must have felt such guilt. All the years that they were together, he had told her very little about himself. The only thing she really wondered about, was why his mother had left, and had never told him she loved him. She promised herself, that her girls would never find out about their father.

His secret life would die with her.